W9-BTF-740

DISCARDED

BRUNO BEAR'S BEDTIME BOOK
Copyright © 1976 by One Strawberry Inc.
All rights reserved
Printed in the United States of America
Library of Congress Catalog Card Number: 76-1500
ISBN: Trade 0-88470-050-X, Library 0-88470-051-8

Bruno Bear's Bedtime Book

A Collection of
Stories and Poems
for the Very Young

Selected and Edited
by Kathleen N. Daly
Illustrated
by Richard Hefter

Strawberry Books • distributed by Larousse & Co., Inc.

for Melissa and Barr

ACKNOWLEDGMENTS

The editor and publisher have made every effort to trace the ownership of all copyrighted material and to secure permission from holders of such work. In the event of any question arising as to the use of any material the publisher and editor, while expressing regret for inadvertent error, will be pleased to make the necessary corrections in future printings. Thanks are due to the following authors, publishers, publications, and agents for permission to use the material indicated.

MARCHETTE CHUTE for "Our Cat" from *Rhymes About Us*. Copyright © 1974 by Marchette Chute. Reprinted by permission of the publishers, E.P. Dutton & Co., Inc.

GERALD DUCKWORTH & CO., LTD., for "The Polar Bear," "The Elephant," and "The Vulture," by Hilaire Belloc from *The Bad Child's Book of Beasts*.

EVANS BROTHERS, LTD., for "Glow-Worms" by P.A. Roper; "The Little Rain" by Mary Coleridge; "The Piffle-Poffle" by Catherine Lodge; "Song of the Whale" author unknown; and "Who Likes the Rain?" author unknown.

ELEANOR FARJEON for "Cats" from *The Children's Bells*. Copyright © 1957 and 1960 by Eleanor Farjeon. Reprinted with permission of the publishers, The Oxford University Press, London, and Henry Z. Walck, a division of David McKay Inc., New York.

DOUGLAS GIBSON for "Cat in Moonlight." Copyright © 1962 by Douglas Gibson.

GINA INGOGLIA for "What Do I See?" Copyright © 1976 by Gina Ingoglia Weiner.

KATHRYN JACKSON for "Big or Little?" Copyright © 1968 by Kathryn Jackson.

ALFRED A. KNOPF, INC., for "The Polar Bear," "The Elephant," and "The Vulture," from *The Bad Child's Book of Beasts* by Hilaire Belloc. Published 1941 by Alfred A. Knopf, Inc.

METHUEN CHILDREN'S BOOKS LTD., for "Ducks' Ditty" by Kenneth Grahame from *The Wind in the Willows*. Text copyright by University Chest Oxford.

THE ESTATE OF DR. ALFRED NOYES and WILLIAM BLACKWOOD & SONS., LTD., for "Daddy Fell into the Pond" by Alfred Noyes.

RANGER RICK'S NATURE MAGAZINE for limericks by David C. Beaty, Grant Baldwin, Linda James, Lynn Jeffries, Fred Kaehler, Claudia Simms, Dave Swartout. Reprinted from RANGER RICK'S NATURE MAGAZINE by permission of the Publisher, National Wildlife Federation.

CHARLES SCRIBNER'S SONS for "Ducks' Ditty" by Kenneth Grahame from *The Wind in the Willows* and for "Pittypat and Tippytoe" by Eugene Field from *Poems of Childhood*.

SHEL SILVERSTEIN for "The Tiger's Tail." Copyright © 1967 by Shel Silverstein.

LOUIS UNTERMEYER for "The Naughty Stars." Copyright © 1976 by Louis Untermeyer.

WESTERN PUBLISHING CO., INC., for "Mother Bear's Helpers" by Patricia M. Scarry. From *The Golden Story Book of River Bend*. Copyright © 1969 by Western Publishing Co., Inc. Reprinted by permission of the publisher.

P.G. WODEHOUSE for "The Thrush." Reprinted by permission of the author's Estate and the author's agents, Scott Meredith Literary Agency, Inc., 845 Third Avenue, New York, New York 10022.

The stories and adaptations by Kathleen N. Daly, "It's All in Your Head," "Song of the Polar Bear," "Goldilocks and the Three Bears," "The Pied Piper of Hamlyn," and "The Three Little Pigs" are Copyright © 1976 by One Strawberry, Inc.

Contents

DISCARDED

A Surprise for Bruno

ONCE there was a bear called Bruno. Bruno lived in Maple Cottage all by himself.

He made his own breakfast (porridge and honey) and tidied his house and went out to do his bits of shopping.

For lunch, if it was fine, he made a honey sandwich and sat in the shade of the big maple tree to eat it and have a little doze. Or he might go fishing or swimming in the pond, or skating in the winter.

At night Bruno made his own supper (perhaps a nice piece of fish and some juicy berries). Then he'd settle down to read until bedtime. And then Bruno would climb into his neat little bed and fall fast asleep.

Bruno was a very happy, very quiet and orderly bear, living all by himself.

One day Tim Turtle, the mailman, brought him a letter.

"Sorry it took so long," said Tim. "I'm not as quick on my feet as I used to be."

Bruno opened the letter and had to sit down very quickly. It was from his sister Bertha, and this is what it said:

Dear Bruno,

Willie and I have just won a quiz competition on TV and they are sending us to the North Pole Hotel for a holiday. Isn't that exciting? I am sending you the children to look after for a couple of weeks, I know you won't mind. They will be arriving Monday.

Love,

Bertha
xxx

10

"Monday!" gasped Bruno. "That's today! Children! Mercy me!"

Poor Bruno was all of a flutter.

Just then the local bus stopped right outside in a cloud of dust.

A small bear in a pink straw hat stepped out. Then came another small bear in a sailor suit. And then came another and another and another until Bruno thought little bears would never stop coming out of that bus.

"Uncle Bruno!" they shouted happily and ran to throw their arms around Bruno.

Bears in chairs, bears on beds, bears in trees, bears in the honey—you never saw so many bears. Bruno kept losing track of how many there were and which one was which, until bedtime. And then suddenly there were five sleepy little bears in five little beds, lying quiet as could be while Bruno began his first bedtime story.

Goldilocks and the Three Bears

"ONCE upon a time there were three bears and they lived in a little cottage in the woods—"

"Just like this one?" asked one little bear.

"Just like this one," said Bruno. "One day—"

"What did the three bears look like?" piped up another little voice.

"There was a great big daddy bear, and a middle-sized mother bear, and a little baby bear. Each morning the three bears got up and had their breakfast—"

"What did they have?" asked one roly-poly bear.

"They had porridge and honey, just like us," said Bruno. "After breakfast they left the cottage and went into the woods. Father Bear went fishing and Mother Bear picked berries and Baby Bear climbed trees and made mud pies and played with rabbits and squirrels—"

"Let's do all those things tomorrow," said Nosy Bear.

"One day," Bruno went on firmly, "the porridge was too hot. So the three bears went for a walk before breakfast. They left the steaming bowls of porridge to cool.

"Now on that very morning a little girl went for a walk in the woods, all by herself, which was very naughty."

"What did she look like?" asked pretty Honey Bear.

"She had curly golden hair and she was called Goldilocks. 'Knock, knock,' she went on the door—"

"Who's there?" giggled Silly Bear.

"When nobody answered," went on Bruno as if he hadn't heard Silly Bear, "she opened the door and walked right in. That was very naughty indeed, but more naughtiness was to come.

"She tried the middle-sized chair. It wasn't right, either.

"She saw the three bowls of porridge. 'Yum, yum.' She tasted porridge from the great big bowl. It was much too hot. She tasted the middle-sized bowl. 'Much too cold.' She tasted the little bowl. It was just right. She ate it all up, every bit."

"Yum, yum," said Roly Bear.

"So then she sat in the little chair and it felt—"

"Just right!" yelled five little voices. Maybe they had heard the story before?

"Right," said Bruno Bear. "But Goldilocks was not just right for the chair. It fell apart and she landed, bump, on the floor.

"Then Goldilocks sat down in the great big chair. It was much too big.

"Then Goldilocks (naughty girl!) went up the little windey staircase. She saw three beds covered with patchwork quilts. Goldilocks decided to take a nap.

"She lay down on the great big bed but it was much too hard. She tried the middle-sized bed but it was much too soft. So she lay on the little bed and it felt—"

"Just right!"

"Right! And Goldilocks fell fast asleep.

16

"When the three bears came home they found the door open. They went in and Father Bear growled in his deep voice, 'SOMEBODY'S BEEN TASTING MY PORRIDGE!'

"And Mother Bear moaned in her middle-sized voice, 'Somebody's been tasting *my* porridge!'

"And Baby Bear said in his little, squeaky voice, 'Somebody's been tasting my porridge and they've eaten it all up, every bit!'

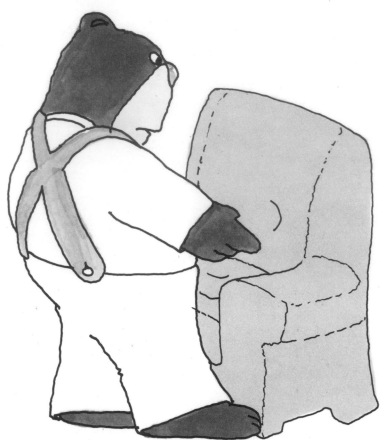

"Baby Bear squeaked, 'Somebody's been sitting in my chair and it's *broken!*'"

"Then Father Bear growled, 'SOMEBODY'S BEEN SITTING IN MY CHAIR!'"

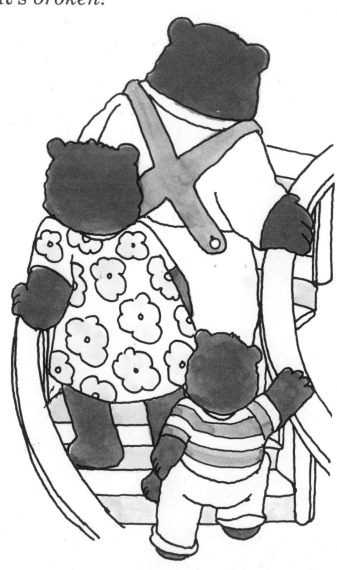

"And Mother Bear moaned, 'Somebody's been sitting in *my* chair!'"

"The three bears climbed up the windey staircase.

"SOMEBODY'S BEEN SLEEP-ING IN MY BED!" growled Father Bear.

"Somebody's been sleeping in my bed, and she's still there!" squeaked Baby Bear.

"Just then Goldilocks woke up. She saw the three bears looking down at her and she squealed with fright. She threw off the patch-work quilt and dashed out the door and down the stairs and out of the cottage and she ran all the way home.

"Somebody's been sleeping in *my* bed!" moaned Mother Bear.

"And nobody even had a chance to say, 'OOOOOH, you naughty girl, you!'"

19

Hungry Little Bears

THE NEXT DAY Bruno and all the little bears went into the woods. They did all the things that little bears are supposed to do.

They climbed trees.

They splashed in the stream.

They flew their kites from a hill-top.

They swung in the hammock.

They found a honeycomb.

And they ate and they ate and they ate.

That night Bruno told them some poems about food and they slept very happily.

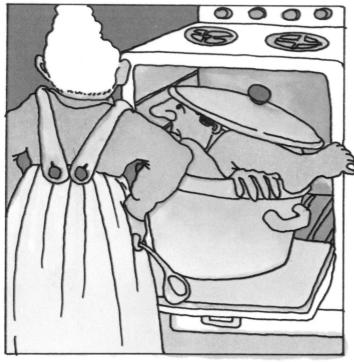

There was an Old Man of Peru,
Who watched his wife making a
    stew;
  But once by mistake,
  In a stove she did bake
That unfortunate Man of Peru.

Edward Lear

If I were an apple
And grew upon a tree,
I think I'd fall down
On a nice bear like me.
I wouldn't stay there
Giving nobody joy;
I'd fall down at once
And say, "Eat me, my boy."

Author Unknown

Mix a pancake,
Stir a pancake,
Pop it in the pan.

Fry the pancake,
Toss the pancake,
Catch it if you can.

Author Unknown

The vulture eats between his meals,
    And that's the reason why
He very, very rarely feels
    As well as you and I.

His eye is dull, his head is bald,
    His neck is growing thinner.
Oh what a lesson for us all
    To only eat at dinner!   *Hilaire Belloc*

There once was a fat little guinea
        pig,
Who cried 'cause he wasn't a
        skinny pig,
He tried to reduce
By living on juice,
And now he's a regular mini-pig.

David C. Beaty

There once was a lady gorilla
Who was fond of the flavor vanilla.
Her husband, it's said
Liked chocolate instead
So he hit her real hard with his pilla

Claudia Simms

Once there was a horse named Nick
Who had a popsicle on a stick.
Along came a boy
Who asked for a toy,
But all he got was a lick.

Grant Baldwin

A Rainy Day

"WHO LIKES THE RAIN?"
grumbled Nosy Bear.
   "Lots of people do," said Bruno
Bear. "Listen."

"I," said the duck. "I call it fun,
For I have my pretty red rubbers
   on;
They make a little three-toed track
In the soft, cool mud—quack!
   quack!"

"I," cried the dandelion, "I—
My roots are thirsty, my buds are
   dry,"

And she lifted a tousled yellow
   head
Out of her green and grassy bed.

Sang the brook, "I welcome every
   drop,
Come down, dear raindrops; never
   stop
Until a broad river you make of
   me,
And then I will carry you to the
   sea."

"I," shouted Ted, "for I can run,
With my high boots and raincoat
   on,
Through every puddle and runlet
   and pool
I find on the road to school."

Author Unknown

When it had stopped raining and
the sun came out, the little bears
went out and shook the tree
branches to see "the little rain."

The great rain is over,
The little rain begun,
Falling from the higher leaves,
Bright in the sun,
Down to the lower leaves,
One drop by one.

Mary Coleridge

Then all the bears came in and
made lots of muddy paw prints.

Paw Prints

"PAW PRINTS, paw prints!" muttered Bruno Bear after a few days had gone by. "It's time I did some housework."

As he scrubbed, he told himself this little poem.

All day long they come and go—
Pittypat and Tippytoe;
Footprints up and down the hall,
Playthings scattered on the floor,
Finger-marks along the wall,
Tell-tale smudges on the door—
By these presents you shall know
Pittypat and Tippytoe.

"Pittypat and Tippytoe, indeed," growled Bruno Bear. "And Silly Bear and Little Bear, and Honey Bear and Nosy Bear and Roly Bear."

That night he told the little bears a story about another Bear family.

Eugene Field

23

"PAW PRINTS!" groaned Mother Bear. She was scrubbing the white wall beside the front door.

"Why are you doing that, Mother?" asked Father Bear, leaning a large, grimy paw against the wall.

"We ought to paint these walls a sticky color so the paw prints won't show," sighed Mother Bear, scrubbing.

Little Richard rested a jammy paw on the wall and said, "Aren't you going to the flower show today, Mother?"

"Yes, she is," said Father. He pulled the string on her apron and said, "You run along and have a nice time, Mother. Little Richard and I will do the walls for you."

Mother Bear was very pleased. She hurried into her hat and waved from the front gate.

"I think you'll be surprised when you get home," called Father Bear with a grin. Then he poured the soapy water into the sink.

"We're not going to scrub Mother's walls. We're going to

24

paint them."

"Oh, I love to paint," said Little Richard.

When Little Richard saw his father begin to paint the wall he said, "I think Mother is going to be very, very surprised!"

Then he copied what his Daddy did. It was lots of fun.

When Mother Bear came home she dropped her pocketbook and gasped, "You've wallpapered the hall!"

"No, we painted it!" grinned Father Bear.

"But it looks like leaves or flowers or something," said Mother. "What a pretty pattern!"

"They're paw prints!" laughed Little Richard. "We colored all the paw prints in different colors. See? The little pink ones are mine."

Mother Bear laughed. Then she hugged her two bears and said, "How clever of you both. It must be the most unusual hallway in the village!"

"And you'll never ask us to keep our paws off the wall again," grinned Little Richard.

Patricia M. Scarry

A Promise

"OH DEAR," said Honey Bear. "We promised we'd be neat and clean. Now look at the mess!"

"Never mind," said Bruno Bear. "Just promise you'll help clean up tomorrow. Now I'll tell you a story about someone—a whole town—that didn't keep a promise. It's called "The Pied Piper of Hamelin.""

ONCE there was a little town called Hamelin, neat and clean as anything. It had lots of happy people and dozens and dozens of children. But one day a terrible thing happened.

RATS!! The rats came to town. All along the streets they ran and into every house. They fought the dogs and cats and everything in sight went down their ratty throats—sugar and spice, hats and coats, bacon and eggs, shoes and socks, pencils and pens—everything.

The people of Hamelin tried every kind of trap they could think of—mouse traps, spring traps, box traps, tiger traps—even rat traps. But the rats escaped every time.

The Mayor and all the people of Hamelin wondered what to do. Suddenly over the squeaking of ten million rats they heard the sweet sound of a pipe. And suddenly all the rats were quiet.

"What's this?" said the Mayor, amazed.

Standing on the corner of the street was a young man playing sweetly on his pipe. All around him sat the rats as quiet as—well, as quiet as mice.

"If you please, sir," said the Piper, "my pipe is magic. I can make the rats follow me wherever I go. For a small sum of money, I will lead them away from Hamelin—"

"A small sum!" screamed the Mayor. "I'll give you a thousand pieces of gold, I promise, if only you'll take them away!"

"Yes, yes!" shouted the people of Hamelin. "Promise him anything!"

So the Piper started to play his magic pipe as he walked off toward the river. And the rats followed him, hurrying, scurrying, whiskers twitching, tumbling, rolling, all the way into the river.

And there they drowned—all gone, down, down to the bottom of the river, hurray!

"Hurray!" shouted the five litle bears.

"Hurray!" shouted all the people of Hamelin. "Let's have a holiday!"

"Great," said the Piper. "But first, please give me my thousand pieces of gold. You promised."

"A thousand pieces of gold!" gasped the Mayor. Then he laughed. "Surely you knew I was joking? Come along, my lad, and join our feast. That's reward enough for you."

"Right!" shouted all the people of Hamelin.

"Wrong," said the Piper. "You have broken your promise, and that is a very bad thing to do, for the Piper must be paid. Now you shall pay."

He took up his pipe again and started to play a different kind of magic tune. Suddenly all along the streets, out from every door, children came—fat children, thin children, rich children, raggedy children, good children, naughty children, dozens and dozens of them. Their fathers and mothers tried to hold them back but the magic was too strong for them. The children followed the Piper, giggling, shouting, leaping, dancing.

All the way out of town they went, and disappeared into a magic door in the mountain and were never seen again. Sometimes, on a quiet night, you can hear music and laughter from inside the mountain. But the people of Hamelin never saw their children again, all because of a broken promise.

Honey Bear looked at the little bears. *"Tomorrow,"* she said, "we'll be neat and clean. And that's a promise."

Some Watery Poems

Everyone grumbled. The sky was grey.
We had nothing to do and nothing to say.
We were nearing the end of a dismal day.
And there seemed to be nothing beyond,
Then
  Daddy fell into the pond!

THE DAY was hot and the little bears went wading to cool off their paws.

And guess who fell into the pond?

Bruno Bear!

And everyone's face grew merry and bright,
And Timothy danced for sheer delight.
"Give me the camera, quick, oh quick!
He's crawling out of the duckweed!" Click!

"All right," he said, wrapped in a huge bath towel. "We'll tell some watery poems."

All along the backwater,
    Through the rushes tall,
Ducks are a-dabbling,
    Up tails all!

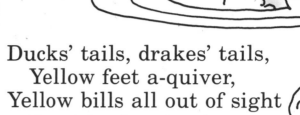

Ducks' tails, drakes' tails,
    Yellow feet a-quiver,
Yellow bills all out of sight
    Busy in the river!

Then the gardener suddenly slapped
    his knee,
And doubled up, shaking silently,
And the ducks all quacked as if
    they were daft
And it sounded as if the old drake
    laughed.
O, there wasn't a thing that didn't
    respond
When
        Daddy fell into the pond!

Slushy green undergrowth
    Where the roach swim,
Here we keep our larder
    Cool and full and dim!

Alfred Noyes

Every one for what he likes!
    We like to be
Heads down, tails up,
    Dabbling free!

High in the blue above
    Swifts whirl and call—
We are down a-dabbling,
    Up tails all!

Kenneth Grahame

If you ever,
        ever,
                ever,
                        ever,
                                ever,
If you ever, ever, ever see a whale,
You must never,
            never,
                    never,
                            never,
You must never tread upon his tail!

If you ever,
        ever,
                ever,
                        ever,
                                ever,
If you ever ever tread upon his tail,
You will never,
            never,
                    never,
                            never,
                                    never,
You will never live to see another whale!

Author Unknown

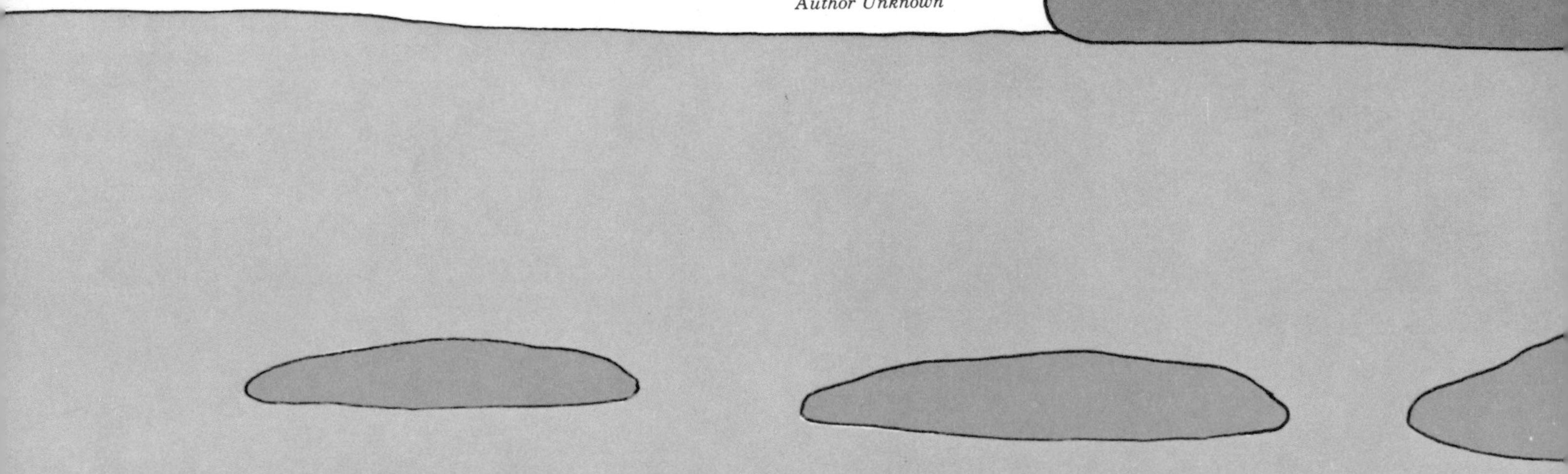

How doth the little crocodile
  Improve his shining tail,
And pour the waters of the Nile
  On every golden scale!

How cheerfully he seems to grin,
  How neatly spread his claws,
And welcome little fishes in,
  With gently smiling jaws!

Lewis Carroll

33

Some Silly Poems

BY NOW everyone was in the mood for some silly poems, and of course, Silly Bear knew lots.

Fuzzy wuzzy was a bear,
Fuzzy wuzzy had no hair.
Fuzzy wuzzy wuzn't fuzzy,
   Wuz he?

Silly Bear

There was an Old Man with a
   beard
Who said, "It is just as I feared—
      Two Owls and a Hen,
      Four Larks and a Wren,
Have all built their nests in my
   beard!"

Edward Lear

34

The polar bear is unaware
Of cold that cuts me through:
For why? He has a coat of hair.
I wish I had one too!

Hillaire Belloc

When people call this beast to
    mind,
They marvel more and more
At such a little tail behind,
So LARGE a trunk before.

Hillaire Belloc

What do I see
Up in the tree?
Apples or peaches or plums?
   NO!
Wrinkled and gray
Singing and gay
A rhino is playing the drums.

What do I smell
Down in the dell?
Flowers or sweet grass or spice?
   NO!
Scaly and green
Grouchy and mean
A dragon is fixing fried rice.

What do I spy
High in the sky?
Lightning or bluebirds or rain?
   NO!
Roaring and proud
Drawing a crowd
A lion is flying a plane.

What do I hear
That's very near?
Elephants, tigers or bears?
   NO!
Noisy with glee
What can it be
It's *you* jumping down the back
   stairs!

Gina Ingoglia

Cats

ONE DAY a cat came to visit the bears in Maple Cottage.

"Now *cats* are very neat and tidy," said Bruno Bear, "with velvet paws and shiny claws, and whiskers twitchy and tails swishy—"

"Cats are warm and dozy," said Honey Bear, as the cat stretched out in the sun and began to purr. "They make me feel cozy. Tell us some cat poems, Uncle Bruno."

Cats sleep
Anywhere,
Any table,
Any chair,
Top of piano,
Window ledge,
In the middle,
On the edge,
Open drawer,
Empty shoe,
Anybody's
Lap will do.
Fitted in a
Cardboard box,
In a cupboard
With your frocks—
Anywhere!
They don't care;
Cats sleep
Anywhere.

Eleanor Farjeon

Through moonlight's milk
She slowly passes
As soft as silk
Between tall grasses.
I watch her go
So sleek and white,
As white as snow,
The moon so bright
I hardly know
White moon, white fur,
Which is the light
And which is her.

The cat goes out
    And the cat comes back
And no one can follow
    Upon her track.
She knows where she's going,
    She knows where she's been,
And all we can do
    Is to let her in.

Marchette Chute

The cat crept away with a yawn
and a stretch and nobody knew
when they would see her next.
That's the way it is, with cats.

39

The Thrush

"NOW I will tell you a beautiful story," said Bruno Bear. "It was first told by a little boy when he was only seven years old. His name was P.G. Wodehouse (his friends called him Plum). When he grew up he wrote lots of funny books about grownups called Jeeves and Bertie Wooster. But when he was seven he wrote about a thrush in the woods. Listen."

ABOUT five years ago in a wood there was a Thrush who built her nest in a poplar tree, and sang so beautifully that all the worms came up from their holes and the ants laid down their burdens, and the crickets stopped their mirth, and moths settled all in a row to hear her. She sang a song as if she were in heaven—going up higher and higher as she sang. At last the song was done and the bird came down panting. Thank you said all the creatures. Now my story is ended.

41

P. G. Wodehouse

Big or Little?

"I SAW a great big enormous bug!" said Little Bear.

"It was not! It was a teeny weeny bug!" said Roly Bear.

>"Eency weency Spider
>Climbed up the water spout.
>Down came the rain drops
>And washed poor Eency out.
>Out came the sunshine
>And dried up all the rain,
>And Eency Weency Spider
>Climbed up that spout again,"

said Silly Bear.

But Little Bear and Roly Bear weren't listening.

"The bug *was* big!" shouted Little Bear.

"It was teeny weeny!" shouted Roly Bear.

"You two remind me of a story," laughed Bruno Bear, "about a big hippopotamus and a little bird."

ONCE there was a tiny little bird who lived on top of a great, enormous, huge, and very big hippopotamus. The two were always together.

But one day, the tiny little bird wanted to take a walk. So he got down and he took a walk.

On his walk he saw a turtle, and a plant with thorns on it, and a round-faced flower.

He saw an animal that darted like a lizard because it was a lizard. And an animal, called a jerboa, that jumped.

He saw an animal that slithered, too.

It was a snake, all right.

"A big, big snake!" cried the tiny little bird, and he flew home as fast as he could fly.

"I saw the biggest snake I ever saw," he told his friend the hippopotamus. "And I saw lots of other big, big things—"

"Is that so?" asked the hippopotamus. "Well, well. I like to see big things, too. So I guess I'll go for a walk."

And he did. On his walk, the great, enormous, huge, and very big hippopotamus saw exactly the same things that the tiny little bird had seen.

He looked and looked at them.

Then he went home shaking his head.

"Did you see them?" asked the tiny little bird.

"Did you see all those big, big things that I saw?"

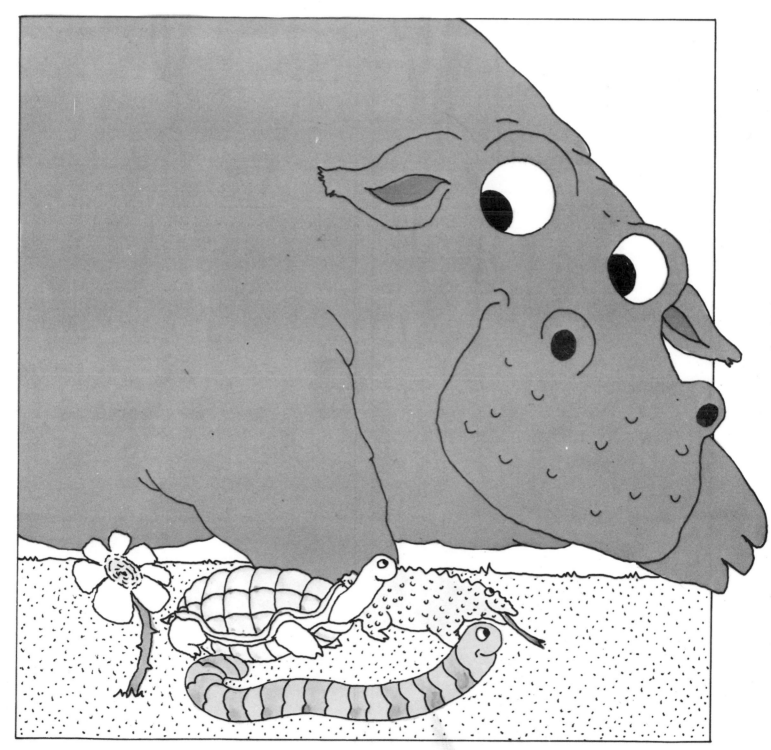

"I saw them all right," the hippopotamus told him. "Only they weren't big, big things—they were little, little, little things."

"They were big, big, big things!" cried the tiny little bird, stamping his tiny little foot.

"Little, little, little things!" snorted the hippopotamus, stamping his enormous foot.

It looked as if those two friends were about to have a brouhaha—which is a fierce, noisy fight.

But just then, the hippopotamus yelled, "Ouch!"

"What's wrong?" asked the tiny little bird.

"Something's biting me," said the hippopotamus. "At least I *think* something is—only it's such a tiny bite that I'm not quite sure."

The tiny little bird flew up on his back.

"Something *is* biting you," he said. "It's a big, big, ugly-looking bug!" And he gobbled it up.

That made the hippopotamus feel so much better that he smiled a great, enormous, huge, and very big smile, and said, "Much obliged."

"My pleasure," smiled the tiny little bird, thinking how good that big ugly-looking bug had tasted.

So the brouhaha was over before it started.

And the great, enormous, huge, and very big hippopotamus and the tiny little bird are the best of friends to this very day.

44

Kathryn Jackson

"And then there's the Piffle-Poffle," said Bruno Bear. "Nobody knows if he's big or small, or really there at all."

If you ever see a creature
With thirty-seven toes
And eyes of an enormous size
And a nose which Grows and
    Grows,
Be on your best behaviour
And treat him with Great Care,
(Which means refrain from laugh-
    ing
At the colour of his hair)
And he might take you home with
    him
To have tea in his lair.
In which case, do not mention
The fact that he is green,
Nor that he is slightly plump
(He likes to think he's lean)
Pretend you haven't noticed
His thirty-seven toes,
And say "How most convenient
To have a nose which grows!"
But never, ever tell him
That his mouth is rather wide
Or you might get a close look at
His reddish-black inside!
If you do not ask him why
He eats without a knife
Then in the Piffle-poffle
You have a friend for life!

Catherine Lodge

45

Spooky Night Stories

ONE NIGHT when everyone in Maple Cottage was in bed Little Bear let out a frightful yell. Everyone woke up.

"What's the matter?" asked Honey Bear.

"I saw a witch, I saw a witch!" said Little Bear.

"It's all in your head," said Bruno Bear. "Listen."

I saw a witch go sailing by,
    go sailing by,
In the dark of night
With no moonlight,
    Sailing by.

Her eyes shone red
And her hair streamed long
And her broom went swish
And her cat went screech.

So I jumped into bed
And shivered and quivered,
    Afraid to look.

Then the moon shone free
And there was light.
The eyes were those of a friendly
    dog,
The hair was the leaves of a wil-
    low tree
And the screech was that of a
    frog.

So I lay in my bed
All snug and warm
And said to the witch,
Get out of my head!

As I was walking up the stair
I met a man who wasn't there.
He wasn't there again today.
I wish, I wish, he'd stay away.

Three little ghostesses,
Sitting on postesses,
Eating buttered toastesses,
Greasing their fistesses,
Up to their wristesses.
Oh, what beastesses
To make such feastesses!

"From ghoulies and ghosties and
long-legged beasties, may the
Good Bear deliver us," said Bruno
Bear.

47

Some Nice Night Stories

IN THE BEGINNING all the stars had their own high places in the heavens. The Star-Minder told them not to move; they were to shine steadily and quietly. But some of the stars grew restless. They would not stay in their places. They ran about and darted across the sky. They made a lot of trouble. They were scolded, but they did not stop being naughty.

One night the Star-Minder decided they had to be punished. They were not allowed to stay in the sky. They could shine only a little while and they had to live the rest of their lives on earth. We see them on summer evenings once in a while. We see their lights flicker on and off as they dart about. They try to get back to heaven but they cannot rise far. They must remain close to earth. We call them fireflies.

48

Louis Untermeyer

With a yellow lantern
  I take the road at night,
And chase the flying shadows
  By its cheerful light.

From the banks and hedgerows
  Other lanterns shine,
Tiny elfin glimmers,
  Not so bright as mine.

Those are glow-worm lanterns,
  Coloured green and blue,
Orange, red and purple,
  Gaily winking through.

See the glow-worms hurry!
  See them climb and crawl!
They go to light the dancers
  At the fairy ball.

P. A. Roper

49

The Song of the Polar Bear

ONE DAY a post card arrived from Bertha and Willie Bear, the little bears' parents.

It came all the way from the North Pole!

There was a picture of lots of white bears with black noses, standing in the snow and waving.

"Brr!" said Little Bear. "It must be cold living up there!"

"No," said Bruno Bear. "It's not cold for Polar bears. I had an uncle in the Arctic and this is what he said:

Polar bears
Sleep in lairs
Warm as bugs in rugs.
It's nice
In the ice
If you're a Polar bear, the king of
  the ice.

Everyone else may freeze,
But the bear doesn't freeze,
He doesn't even sneeze.
In his white fur coat
He's known to float
In the waters dark and cold,
Singing a song, an Arctic song,
That goes like this:

"Oh this is the land
  where I was born
Where ice and snow
And the old ice floe
And the bergy hills
And the frosty rills
Are home to me.
Isn't it nice, I'm king of the ice!

50

This is the land that's never warm—
No honey for me,
No berries or nuts.
The herring and cod
Don't taste odd.
An occasional seal
Makes a whale of a meal,
Oh this is the land for me—
Isn't it nice, I'm king of the ice!"

Without a reel
He'll catch a fish,
A tasty dish,
For his evening meals.
He'll frighten off seals,
Singing a song, an Arctic song.

The white wolves hunt
By the light of the moon
And the cry of the loon.
The Eskimo child
To his mother's croon
Falls asleep in the Arctic deep.

Then the Polar bear
Comes out from his lair
And pads in the snow
Of the lone ice floe,
Singing a song, an Arctic song:

"Oh this is the land
where I was born
Where ice and snow
And the old ice floe
And the bergy hills
And the frosty rills
Are home to me.
Isn't it nice, I'm king of the ice!

This is the land that's never warm
No honey for me
No berries or nuts.
The herring and cod
Don't taste odd.
An occasional seal
Makes a whale of a meal,
Oh this is the land for me—
Isn't it nice, I'm king of the ice!"

"Just think," sighed Roly Bear, "ice cream never melts up there, in the North Pole."

"Popsicles hang from the cliffs!" said Honey Bear.

"And there are snowballs all year long!" said Little Bear.

"I had an uncle in Alaska," said Silly Bear.

"Nome?" asked Bruno Bear.

"Of course I know him!"

"I mean," said Bruno, "in the town of Nome, Alaska?"

"I'd know him *any*where," said Silly Bear. "He's been in the family for ages."

"Oh, *silly* bear," everyone groaned.

More Silly Poems

"I SUPPOSE you know more silly stories," said Nosy Bear.

"You bet," said Silly Bear.

There was a bear,
He had a lot of hair.
One day he started to mow
Himself from head to toe,
And now he is bare.

Linda James

There was a young mouse named
   Toot,
Who lived in a brown leather boot.
Every night he came out,
When no one was about,
And played on his cute little flute.

Lynn Jeffries 53

Everybody groaned and giggled.
"More, more!" yelled Little Bear,
rolling around on the floor.
"There are guppies and puppies
and a bat named Hugh," said Silly
Bear. "Listen."

There once were six little puppies.
They knocked down a bowlful of
　　　guppies.
When the little fish
Fell out of the dish,
You couldn't tell guppies from
　　　puppies!

Fred Kaehler

54

There once was a bat named Hugh,
Who wanted something to do.
So he flew out of his steeple,
And scared all the people,
And then he flew off to Peru!

David Swartout

"Just one more," pleaded Nosy Bear.
"All right," said Bruno Bear. "One more."

55

Oh who will wash the tiger's ears?
And who will comb his tail?
And who will brush his sharp
    white teeth?
And who will file his nails?

Oh Bobby may wash the tiger's
    ears
And Susy may file his nails
And Lucy may brush his long
    white teeth
And I'll go down for the mail.

   "Now off you go to wash ears and
tails, teeth and nails,"said Bruno,
"It's bedtime."

Shel Silverstein

56

The Three Little Pigs

"ISN'T IT suppertime yet?" asked Roly Bear.

"What, hungry again?" said Bruno Bear. He was chopping berries and roots to make a delicious honey stew. "Sit down and I'll tell you about a wolf who *really* got hungry. He got himself tangled up with three little pigs."

"ONCE upon a time there were three little pigs.

"One of them was a merry little soul and thought life was jolly.

"The second little pig was bad tempered and thought that life was terrible.

"The third little pig was very sensible and said, 'Now, what are we all going to do?'

"'I will dance and sing,' said the first little pig. So he danced and sang and he had a lovely time. But one day a large character came knocking at his door. This character had big black teeth..."

"He didn't go to his dentist often enough," said Honey Bear.

"Right. He was a wolf. A big, bad wolf. 'I am going to eat you up,' said the wolf.

"'Tra la, how silly you are,' said the little pig. He got out his guitar and he danced and he sang so merrily that the wolf couldn't help joining in. But pretty soon he got hungry. 'Little pig,' he said, 'you are so merry and gay that I cannot eat you up. But I am hungry, so I must go on my way.'

"So the wolf went on his way and he came to the house of the second little pig. He knocked on the door.

"'Go away,' the little pig said. 'You are a stranger. My mom told me not to talk to strangers. And that means you.'

"Angrily the wolf huffed and puffed until he had blown the house down. He was just about to eat up the second little pig.

"But the first little pig came running, playing his guitar and singing and the wolf, bad as he was, and hungry as he was, didn't have the heart to eat up the second little pig.

"'Oh blow,' he said angrily. 'Huff and puff,' he said. 'I am sick of little pigs. And I am hungry. No more guitars. No more singing and dancing. That kind of thing doesn't fill a wolf's empty stomach.'

"'Try spinach and cream,' sang the happy little pig. 'Cream! Ice cream! Mellow jellow, potatoes, tomatoes, cabbage and figs, who wants pigs?'

"But the wolf was already on his way, huffing and puffing and snorting angrily, 'Pigs! The next one I see, I eat. I'm *hungry*.'

"He came to the house of the third little pig.

"Now the third little pig was a very clever little pig and he knew exactly what to do.

"'All right,' he said. 'You are hungry. So are we. I'm going to cook a meal you'll never forget. It's what pigs love to eat. After we have all eaten, if you are still hungry, you can eat us all up. Okay?'

"'Okay,' said the wolf. 'What's on the menu?'

"'There are roasted rats and spiced gnats, poached roaches in coaches of bread and mold, and ants in pants (icy cold), and fiery faggots swarming with maggots, and leeches in dirty breeches, and slugs (slimy) and bugs (grimy) and fleas in sleeves and ...'

"'Stop, stop!' yelled the wolf, running for the door. 'Now that I know what you little pigs eat I don't want you any more. No sir. It's good-bye for me.'

"The big bad wolf sped off in a cloud of dust. He never bothered the little pigs again. But he came back on birthdays and holidays and had spinach and cream, ice cream, mellow jellow, potatoes and tomatoes, cabbage and figs—but no pigs.

"And they all lived happily ever after."

Good-bye, Little Bears!

"ALL RIGHT," said Bruno Bear, "I want you all to get busy. We are going to have a party tomorrow—because you are going away, back home to your mom and dad."

Honey Bear began to sob.

Silly Bear began to sob.

Bruno Bear brushed back a tear, very bravely.

"Now, now," he said. "No crying, please. We must plan the party."

"Balloons," said Silly Bear right away.

"Balloons, hats, the works," said Bruno Bear.

And so they strung up balloons, and made cakes and ice cream, and invited all their friends—squirrels and rabbits and bats (everyone wore hats), and mice and moles and voles, and Tim Turtle, the mailman, and spiders and grasshoppers and partyhoppers—you never saw such a crowd.

When it was time to say good-bye, the little bears had their suitcases packed. They were all lined up and ready for the bus.

"Good-bye,"said Bruno Bear.

"May we come again?" asked Honey Bear.

"Yes," said Bruno Bear with a smile. "Meanwhile, I'll have all those paw prints to remember you by!"

And do you know, Bruno Bear has never washed those paw prints away, to this very day?